Penny-Farthing Productions Presents

AUDREY'S MAGIC NINE

The Pencil and the Dream

Created by
Courtney Huddleston

Written by
Michelle Wright

Art by
**Courtney Huddleston
&
Francesco Gerbino**

Colors by
Tracy Bailey

Letters by
André McBride

Penny-Farthing Productions, Inc.

Publisher
Ken White, Jr.

Editor-In-Chief
Marlaine Maddux

Creative Director
Trainor Houghton

Project Director
Courtney Huddleston

**Senior Editor and
Marketing Coordinator**
Julia Ahadi

Assistant Editor
Jamie Luu Murphy

Graphic Designer
André McBride

Corporate Office Manager
Pam Johnston

Accounts Manager
Selma Medina

Chapter Five

Center of Gravity

I'M LATE FOR THE AIKIDO DEMONSTRATION, ASA!

IF I'M LATE...

... THEN TABITHA AND JONATHAN WILL BE *SOOO* DISAPPOINTED IN ME.

OH, LASS.

I KNOW THEY'RE GOOD PEOPLE, BUT I THINK THEY RUN YOU RAGGED JUST TO IMPRESS THEIR "FRIENDS"...

...AND BY FRIENDS I MEAN A PACK OF JACKALS. NASTY CRITTERS.

YOU KNOW, I THINK THEY HAVE JACKALS ON JUST ABOUT EVERY WORLD.

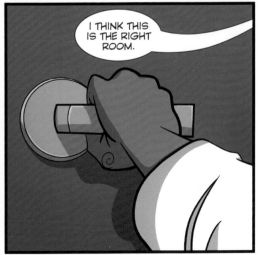

I THINK THIS IS THE RIGHT ROOM.

SO, THE QUESTION IS, SKIPPY...

...ARE YOU IN OR OUT?

OK.

YOU HAVE TO ANSWER THE QUESTION.

ARE YOU *IN* OR *OUT*?

OK.

NO! YOU HAVE TO CHOOSE--

OWWWW!

POW

ASA, THIS IS IT.

I'M AS SCARED AS IF THE NIGHT NOISE WERE HERE.

DON'T BE.

WOW!

YOU CAN SAY THAT AGAIN.

WOW!

TODAY WE MEET FOR A VERY SPECIAL DEMONSTRATION...

...TO SEE HOW AIKIDO ALLOWS A SMALL GIRL TO...

...USE CENTER OF GRAVITY TO OVERCOME A LARGER OPPONENT.

DO YOU REMEMBER WHAT IT WAS LIKE BEFORE THIS KID CAME ALONG?

YOU COULD LAUGH AT JONATHAN'S CHICKEN LEGS...

...AND TABITHA'S BIG REAR END WITHOUT ANY GUILT WHATSOEVER.

I THOUGHT AUDREY WOULD JUST BE SOME RANDOM ADOPTED KID WE COULD MAKE FUN OF JUST LIKE WE MADE FUN OF TABITHA AND JONATHAN.

I TRIED FOR A WHILE, BUT EVEN THOUGH SHE'S REALLY INTO PUPPETS...

...SHE'S ACTUALLY GOOD AT STUFF. SO, YOU CAN'T REALLY SAY A WORD.

YEAH.

BECAUSE SAYING SOMETHING GOOD ABOUT AUDREY...

...IS LIKE SAYING SOMETHING GOOD ABOUT TABITHA AND JONATHAN.

AND WHY WOULD WE DO *THAT?*

THEY'RE JUST LAME WANNABES USING THAT KID TO BE POPULAR.

WE HAVE TO LEAVE.

WHA—

DUE TO A FAMILY EMERGENCY...WE WILL HAVE TO CONCLUDE TODAY'S DEMONSTRATION.

LET'S GIVE THESE KIDS A ROUND OF APPLAUSE.

CLAP

CLAP

CLAP

CLAP

CLAP

CLAP

CLAP

DIDN'T I DO A GOOD JOB, TABITHA?

YOU WERE SUBLIME, HONEY.

IT'S JUST TIME TO GO.

BUT—

TAB, WHAT'S THE MATTER?

WHAT DO YOU MEAN, "WHAT'S THE MATTER?"

DIDN'T YOU HEAR MISTY AND HER LITTLE COVEN? WE'RE JUST "LAME WANNABES."

WELL...

...YES...I DID HEAR THEM SAY IT. SO?

SO?!

YOU'RE OK WITH THAT?

BUT I THOUGHT THIS IS WHAT YOU WANTED?

WHAT WE WANTED.

WHAT? TO BE ABUSED BY OUR SO-CALLED FRIENDS?

NO. TO BE HAZED UNTIL THEY ACCEPTED US.

OH MY GOSH.

WE REALLY ARE LAME.

8

HONEY, HERE'S A LITTLE MONEY IF YOU FIND SOMETHING.

WE'RE JUST A BLOCK FROM THE HOUSE, SO IF YOU WANT TO STAY LONGER THAN US, YOU CAN.

OK.

I'VE NEVER SEEN SO MANY TREASURES.

NEITHER HAVE I.

SO, WE'VE GOT CLOCKS, ROBOTS...

WELL, WILL YA LOOK AT THAT?

AN ODDLY FAMILIAR, MOUSE...

...TABITHA AND JONATHAN HAVING A NICE CONVERSATION...

...A STRANGE BOY...

IT'S OPON!

WHAT DO WE HAVE HERE?

THAT'S...UH...A PUPPET...I'VE BEEN LOOKING FOR.

OH, REALLY?

SO, YOU THINK IT'S SPECIAL, RIGHT?

YES.

IT'S VERY SPECIAL.

HOW MUCH FOR THE PUPPET?

ONE DOLLAR.

SOLD.

HEY! THAT'S NOT FAIR.

FAIR?

YOU ALREADY HAVE THREE PUPPETS. WHY CAN'T I HAVE ONE?

THAT PUPPET IS IMPORTANT. YOU DON'T UNDERSTAND.

I DO UNDERSTAND. NOW I HAVE A PUPPET, TOO.

...

AW, I RUINED IT.

WHO ME?

YEAH YOU.

I'LL FIGHT YOU FOR THAT PUPPET!

REALLY?

OK.

WHEN?

RIGHT NOW!

AROUND THE SIDE OF THE HOUSE.

WHENEVER YOU'RE READY.

NO, WHENEVER YOU'RE READY.

OH, IS YOUR PUPPET GOING TO GET ME.

YEAH.

I MEAN...

...MAYBE.

CRASH!

STERK...?

I CAN DO THIS!

I'LL RALLY!

HERE, LET ME HELP YOU...

...JUST TO BE FAIR.

BINK

BINK

BINK

BINK

BINK

THIS KEEPS GETTING WORSE AND WORSE.

MY POWERS DON'T WORK.

THEY DON'T WORK AT ALL.

HEY YOUNG MAN...

...PICK ON SOMEONE YOUR OWN SIZE!

BUT—I—I—

AND YOU...

...NEXT TIME GIVE THAT BOY SOMETHING TO THINK ABOUT.

BACK ON VORGON...I WOULD HAVE...AND THEN... AND THEN....

I WAS A *WARRIOR.*

WHAT DO WE DO NOW?

IT'S HARD FOR ME TO ACT IN DAYLIGHT, YEAH.

PEEPS MIGHT SEE.

SAME HERE.

STERK?

ANY HELP FROM VORGON'S #1 WARRIOR?

LOOK, STERK. IT'S HARD TO DEAL WITH DIMINISHED POWER, BUT WE CAN STILL HELP.

YEAH, BRUV.

I AIN'T GOT A TENTH OF ME ABILITIES, BUT I CAN DO SOMETHING.

YOU GOT THIS, KID.

YOU GOT THOSE SKILLS YOU USED TODAY. YOU JUST GOT TO HAVE SOME CONFIDENCE. YOU ARE SMALL AND WILY, USE THOSE TO YOUR ADVANTAGE.

THE ONLY TIME I ALMOST GOT LICKED WAS BY A LITTLE OL' MARSH CRITTER.

I COULD TAKE EVERY GIANT VORGON THREW AT ME.

AND I WAS THE VORGON ARM JOUSTING CHAMPION FOR TEN LUNAR YEARS IN A ROW.

ALMOST THE CHAMPION FOR TEN LUNAR YEARS IN A ROW.

BUT THAT CRITTER GOT TO ME BECAUSE I UNDERESTIMATED IT.

I LEARNED AN IMPORTANT LESSON ABOUT LITTLE MARSH CRITTERS THAT DAY.

AND I LEARNED A LITTLE ABOUT MY OWN EGO.

WHY DIDN'T I JUST GIVE HER THE PUPPET.

STUPID!

HEY YOU!

I'M SO GLAD TO SEE...

...AHEM...THAT YOU'VE COME BACK TO GET YOUR TAIL KICKED AGAIN.

I HAVE COME BACK FOR THAT PUPPET.

AND HOW IS THAT GOING TO HAPPEN?

COME AND SEE.

BY THE WAY, MY NAME IS BACKWARD.

NO, THAT'S NOT RIGHT.

I'M BREAKIT... NO... BECOME...NO... BARKER... *AH!*

MY...NAME... IS...BECKETT.

WHEW!

NICE TO MEET YOU, BECKETT!

I'M AUDREY, AND I'LL SEE YOU LATER.

I LOVE YOU.

I CAN'T WAIT TO GET TO KNOW YOU.

ALL I'M SAYING IS THAT WE MADE A DECISION TO NEVER BE RIDICULED AGAIN.

AND WE HAVEN'T BEEN SINCE.

YES, WE HAVE.

BEHIND OUR BACKS, WELL NOT EVEN BEHIND OUR BACKS, THOSE PEOPLE—

HEY, SWEETIE.

DID YOU FIND SOMETHING NICE?

I...DID....

WHAT IS *THIS?*

OH...JONATHAN STRESS BAKES WHEN HE'S NERVOUS.

IT'LL BE OK.

WHY DON'T YOU GO TO YOUR ROOM, AND WE'LL BRING YOU SOME GOODIES.

SURE.

Chapter Six

O Fortuna

ARE YOU READY?

YES!

OH...MY...GOSH!

I'VE NEVER BEEN TO A CARNIVAL BEFORE!

AND IT GETS BETTER.

NOW, JONATHAN AND I CAN'T RIDE RIDES.

OUR TUMMIES ARE TOO IFFY.

BUT WE WILL BE RIGHT HERE.

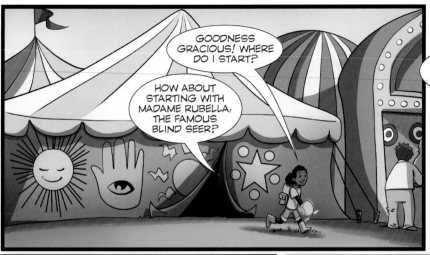

GOODNESS GRACIOUS! WHERE DO I START?

HOW ABOUT STARTING WITH MADAME RUBELLA, THE FAMOUS BLIND SEER?

WHO SAID THAT?

I DID, DEAR. I AM MADAME RUBELLA, THE FAMOUS BLIND SEER.

I'M IN THE TENT.

COME INSIDE AND DISCOVER YOUR DESTINY.

WOW!

HUMPH!

I THINK WE SHOULD LEAVE.

I CANNOT SEE, UNFORTUNATELY, BUT WHILE FATE HAS RENDERED ME SIGHTLESS, IT HAS ALSO GIVEN ME THE ABILITY TO SENSE THE FORTUNES OF OTHER PEOPLE.

IF YOU'D LIKE, I'LL READ YOURS FOR FREE.

I CAN ALREADY SENSE THAT YOU ARE AN ORIGINAL. THERE IS NO ONE ELSE QUITE LIKE YOU.

AHEM! DON'T TAKE ME OFF YOUR H—

REALLY?

REALLY, MY DEAR.

ARE YOU READY, DEAR?

OH...UH...YES.

WELL, THEN, I NEED YOU TO CLOSE YOUR EYES AND ENVISION ANY QUESTIONS YOU MAY HAVE, SO THE REAL WORK CAN BEGIN.

THINK VERY HARD.

I AM.

31

GOOD, DEAR.

NOW, KEEP THOSE EYES CLOSED TIGHT.

I WILL NEED A FEW MINUTES TO DELVE INTO YOUR SOUL.

OH...MY...

...THIS IS ABSOLUTELY—

IS SOMETHING WRONG?

OH NO, DEAR.

I AM JUST ENJOYING YOUR ABSOLUTELY AMAZING AURA.

OH, OK.

NOW, MY DEAR, I SEE THAT YOU ARE PERHAPS CONCERNED THAT TWO FRIENDS FIGHT CONSTANTLY.

YES! HOW DID—

KEEP YOUR EYES CLOSED!

SORRY!

IT'S OK, DEAR, BUT WE MUST STAY FOCUSED.

YES, MA'AM.

YOU VERY MUCH WANT YOUR TWO FRIENDS TO GET ALONG, BUT THEY REFUSE.

IS THIS CORRECT?

YES, IT IS.

AND YOU WOULD LIKE TO KNOW HOW TO MAKE YOUR FRIENDS MEND THEIR WAYS?

EXACTLY.

ALL RIGHT, DEAR.

YOU MAY OPEN YOUR EYES.

FOR THE MINIMAL PRICE OF TWENTY DOLLARS, I WILL TELL YOU HOW.

BUT YOU SAID IT WAS *FREE*.

IT WAS, BUT IN ORDER TO HELP YOU NOW, I REQUIRE FINANCIAL ASSISTANCE TO SOLVE YOUR VERY DIFFICULT PROBLEM.

I CAN DO TEN DOLLARS.

I'M SORRY. NO.

BUT, YOU WOULDN'T HAPPEN TO HAVE ANY PUPPETS WOULD YOU?

WHY, NO DEAR.

OK. THANK YOU.

FIVE?

NOPE.

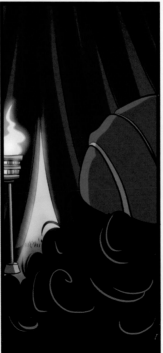

THAT WAS DISAPPOINTING. SHE SEEMED VERY NICE AT FIRST.

I SHOULDN'T HAVE TAKEN YOU OFF MY HAND.

WELL, NOW YOU KNOW.

SHE WAS RIGHT ABOUT NEMA AND OPON, THOUGH.

MAYBE. MAYBE NOT.

BUT I HAVE BEEN THINKING ABOUT HOW TO GET THOSE TWO TO RIGHTS.

HOW?

PUT ME AWAY A WHILE, LASS

THEN LET THEM BOTH EXPERIENCE THIS WONDER. WE'LL SEE IF THAT DOESN'T FIX THEM.

IF WE ARE TO FIND ANY OTHER MEMBERS OF THE NINE, WE NEED THEM CORDIAL.

IT WOULD LOOK BAD IF THEY WEREN'T GETTING ALONG.

OK....

HERE GOES NOTHING.

HELLO, NEMA.

HALLO YA-SELF.

NO!

WE ARE AT A CARNIVAL, A SPECIAL PLACE, A PLACE TO GET OVER THIS PROBLEM YOU TWO HAVE.

I AIN'T GOT NO PROBLEM.

NOR DO I.

STOP!

WE AREN'T DOING THIS TODAY.

THIS IS WHAT IS GOING TO HAPPEN.

YOU TWO ARE GOING TO HAVE A GOOD TIME, WHETHER YOU LIKE IT OR NOT.

HISS!

HMPH!

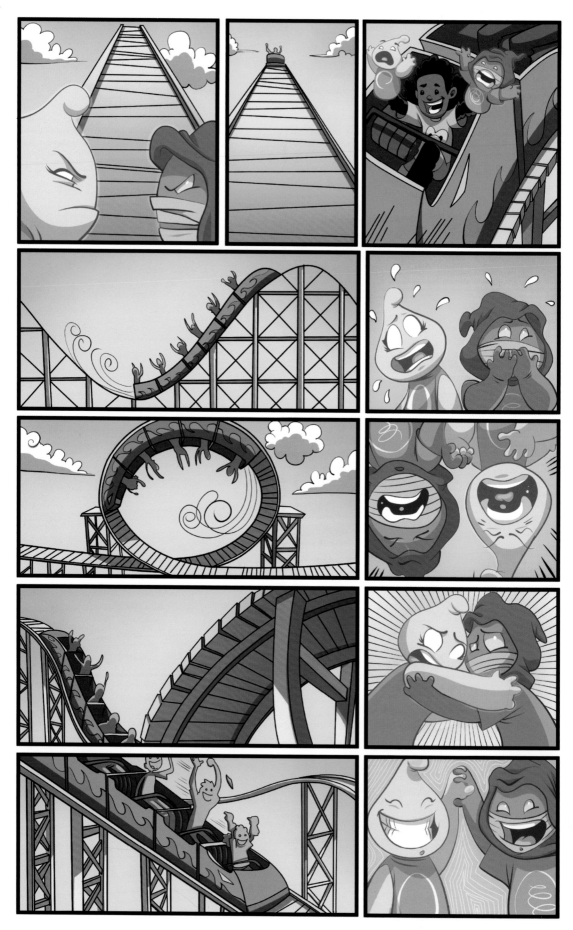

GASP!

WHY CAN'T YOU GUYS GET ALONG?

YOU'RE MEMBERS OF THE NINE, AFTER ALL.

OUR PROBLEM GOES BACK CENTURIES.

YEAH.

 MY PEOPLE, THE DOSOJINN SETTLED THE ENTIRE SOUTHERN REGION OF VORGON'S MAIN CONTINENT—SAGUENAY—UP TO THE MIGHTY RIVER MELUSINE. WE FOUNDED THE CAPITOL CITY, CAVIRA.

 NO, THA'S NOT RIGHT!

THE AMUNET ALREADY SETTLED THE NORTH BY THE TIME THE LIKES OF YOU ARRIVED, DIDN'T WE?

CAVIRA WAS *OUR PLACE.*

THE DOSOJINN TRIED TO STEAL IT.

NO, WE SIMPLY WANTED FRIENDLY NEGOTIATION.

BUT IT DIDN'T TURN OUT THAT WAY.

BEFORE THE COUNCIL OF NINE, THE WIZARDS SOMETIMES STEPPED INTO TO HELP IN DISPUTES.

THEY MADE US SHARE CAVIRA AND THE RIVER.

AND WE AIN'T GOT ALONG SINCE.

THANK YOU, LITTLE GIRL. I THOUGHT I LOST THIS LITTLE GEM WHEN IT BLEW OUT OF MY HANDS.

BUT—

IT'S SOMETHING ELSE, HUH? MAKES YOU FEEL HAPPY.

CAN YOU BELIEVE THAT MADAME RUBELLA, THE FAMOUS BLIND SEER DREW *THIS?*

SUCH IMAGINATION! SUCH SKILL!

AND SHE'S BLIND!

AMAZING!

WAIT...UH...MR. WOLF BOY. DID YOU SAY MADAME RUBELLA?

YEAH. SHE'S SELLING THEM.

MY GIRLFRIEND GOT ONE, TOO.

IF YOU WANT ONE, YOU BETTER HURRY.

EVERYONE'S GETTING THEM.

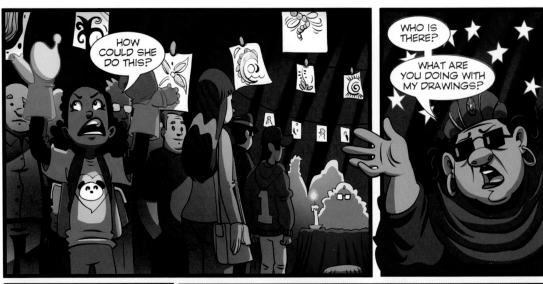

NOW, MY GIRL, DON'T PULL ANOTHER HAIR OVER THIS.

I'VE GOT A PLAN.

I DON'T SEE HOW IT'LL WORK.

THE CARNIVAL PEOPLE ARE PROTECTING HER.

AND SHE *CAN* SEE.

SHE'S A FAKE AND...A...A...

A WUD. THAT'S WHAT SHE IS.

A WUD!

DON'T TEACH HER THAT LANGUAGE.

YOU SHOULD HEAR WHAT ASA HAS TAUGHT HER.

I DON'T EVEN WANT TO KNOW.

WELL, I THINK WE SHOULD WORK ON REVEALING RUBELLA FOR WHAT SHE IS.

OPON! THAT WAS AMAZING.

HOW DID YOU DO IT?

YEAH, OPON? DO TELL.

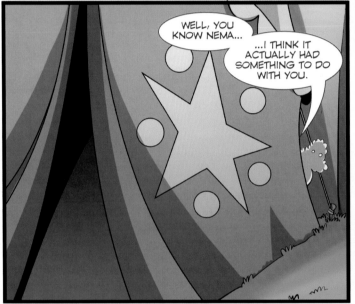

WELL, YOU KNOW NEMA...

...I THINK IT ACTUALLY HAD SOMETHING TO DO WITH YOU.

HOW DO YOU MEAN?

I THINK YOUR RIDICULE DID THE TRICK.

I AM ACTUALLY STRONGER IN THIS PUPPET FORM WHEN YOU INSULT ME.

SO, NEMA, WOULD YOU MIND—

MOCKING OPON? LET'S GO.

HELP! SOMEONE HELP ME!

MADAME RUBELLA, ARE YOU OK?

LOOK AT HER! JUST LOOK AT HER.

SHE JUST APPEARED OUT OF NOWHERE JUST TO SCARE ME LIKE SHE HAD SOME SORT OF POWER OR SOMETHING.

MADAME RUBELLA, ARE YOU SAYING...

...THAT YOU CAN SEE?

I... UH... WELL... HEH.

WHAT IS THE MEANING OF THIS?

A MAN TOLD ME YOU SOLD HIM THIS, BUT THIS IS MY DAUGHTER'S ART.

IT'S NOT YOURS TO SELL!

JUST A LITTLE MISUNDERSTANDING IS ALL.

NO HARD FEELINGS, HUH, DEAR?

MA'AM, THIS REALLY HURT ME.

I'M VERY SORRY, BUT WAIT, I CAN MAKE IT UP TO YOU...

...REMEMBER, YOU ASKED ME FOR SOMETHING ELSE WHEN YOU SAW ME.

I ASKED IF YOU HAD PUPPETS...

NAJA!

I HOPE SHE'LL TAKE SOME OF YOUR HURT AWAY.

LATER THAT NIGHT.

SO, NAJA. YOU REALLY CAN SEE IN THE DARK?

ON VORGON — YES. MY PEOPLE LIVED IN PERPETUAL NIGHT.

BUT, HERE I CANNOT SAY JUST HOW EFFECTIVE THAT ABILITY WILL BE.

WELL, CONSIDERING OPON'S EXPERIENCE TODAY...

...WE NEVER KNOW WHAT'S GOING TO HAPPEN.

SNAAAAAAAA

WHAT WAS THAT?

WE DON'T KNOW.

WELL, I THINK WE SHOULD SEE WHAT IT IS FOR OURSELVES.

WHO IS WITH ME?

SNAAAAA!

53

Chapter Seven
The Hinkles Strike Back

WHAT'S WRONG?

OH...

...YEAH.

WELL, YOU FOUND US OUT.

THIS IS WHO WE *REALLY* ARE.

WHY DO YOU GUYS COVER UP WHO YOU REALLY ARE?

WELL...

HA! HA! HA! HA! HA! HA! HA! HA!

ACK!

GORILLA!

...THAT'S A LONG STORY.

HA! FOUR EYES!

HA! FREAK FEET!

HA! ACCORDION PLAYER!

BUT, YOU GUYS ARE AWESOME AS YOU ARE!

REALLY?

OF COURSE!

I THINK IT IS SO COOL THAT YOU HAVE SIX TOES.

I HAD EXTRA FINGERS ON MY HANDS, TOO, BUT MY PARENTS HAD THEM REMOVED.

PEOPLE WERE UNKIND.

WELL, I'M GLAD TO HAVE PARENTS WHO ARE SO UNIQUE!

YOU'RE LIKE NO ONE ELSE IN THE ENTIRE WORLD.

GULP

WHAT'S THE MATTER?

WE COULD NEVER DO *THAT*.

NEVER.

THOSE PEOPLE...

...WOULDN'T UNDERSTAND.

THAT IS *EXACTLY* WHY YOU SHOULD GO!

SURE, THEY WOULD BE SHOCKED.

64

AND SURE SOMEONE MIGHT LAUGH.

BUT THAT PERSON WOULD BE JUST TRYING TO COVER UP SOMETHING THEY ARE EMBARRASSED OF, TOO.

AND IF PEOPLE STILL LAUGH, WELL THAT'S THEIR PROBLEM, NOT YOURS.

I'M AFRAID IT'S NOT THAT SIMPLE.

WE'D BE LUCKY TO GET OUT ALIVE.

KNOCK KNOCK KNOCK

SEE, JUST TALKING ABOUT THEM MAKES THEM APPEAR.

IT MAKES THEM STRONGER, TOO.

IT'S OK TABITHA.

IF YOU DON'T MAKE EYE CONTACT, THEY CAN'T HURT YOU.

I HAVE A FLOWER DELIVERY FOR SOMEONE NAMED TABITHA.

THAT'S ME.

JUST SIGN RIGHT HERE.

LOVE YOUR GLASSES BY THE WAY!

OH, THANK YOU.

WHERE HAVE I SEEN HER BEFORE?

I REMEMBER NOW!

SNAP

AND YOU...

...NEXT TIME GIVE THAT BOY SOMETHING TO THINK ABOUT.

SHE HAS ELDURA!

66

I HAVE TO GO!

WHERE ARE YOU...

...GOING?

HOTEL

WHAT DO WE DO?

MAYBE WE CAN CONTACT THAT FLORIST...

...AND SEE IF THEY CAN REACH THE DRIVER.

GOOD IDEA.

THIS IS GOING TO BE EASIER THAN I THOUGHT.

I NEED YOUR HELP, ASA.

LASS, I CANNOT DO IT.

THIS IS TOO DANGEROUS.

BUT, SHE'S *RIGHT THERE.*

WE NEED TO GET ELDURA!

WE'LL HAVE ANOTHER CHANCE.

BESIDES, OUT OF ALL OF THE NINE, ELDURA IS THE MOST CAUTIOUS.

SHE WOULD WANT YOU TO BE CAUTIOUS, TOO.

ROOOAAAARR!

IN FACT, SHE'S FAMOUS FOR HER RESTRAINT, EVEN IN THE MOST TERRIFYING OF CIRCUMSTANCES.

DRIP DRIP

ROAR?

BUT HER LIMIT...

...WAS WHEN ONE CREATURE HARMED ANOTHER, IN ANY WAY.

THOSE WERE THE SORT OF OFFENSES...

...THAT MADE ELDURA ALL FLAMEY.

AUDREY?

AUDREY, ARE YOU EVEN LISTENING TO ME?

OH MY GOSH!

MISS HINKLE?

YOU SEE, LASS.

IT'S *HER!*

AUDREY, I NEED YOU TO GET OFF THE STREET RIGHT NOW!

OK.

I'VE BEEN FOLLOWING YOU ALL OVER TOWN.

I KNOW.

YOUR PARENTS CALLED MY COMPANY. THEY ARE VERY WORRIED.

THERE ARE MY PARENTS NOW.

I'M GLAD THEY DIDN'T DILLYDALLY.

AUDREY!

YOU JUST CAN'T TAKE OFF LIKE THAT.

I KNOW WHAT SHE WAS AFTER.

SHE WANTED THIS PUPPET.

AUDREY—

IT'S OK.

AUDREY, I'M GIVING THIS TO YOU SO YOU'LL REMEMBER NOT TO SCARE THE PEOPLE WHO CARE FOR YOU.

THANK YOU!

SURE THING.

WOW! SHE WAS REALLY—

BUT THE NEXT TIME IT HAPPENS I'M CALLING SOCIAL SERVICES.

OH... WELL... THERE IT IS.

I'M SORRY I RAN OFF LIKE THAT...

OH, AUDREY THIS ISN'T YOUR FAULT. THIS IS OURS. WE HAVEN'T BEEN AS...

...ATTENTIVE AS WE SHOULD BE LATELY.

PERHAPS WE HAVE PUSHED YOU A BIT TOO HARD TO PROPEL OUR OWN SOCIAL AMBITIONS.

YOU TOOK OFF TODAY FOR A PUPPET, OF ALL THINGS...AND WE DIDN'T EVEN STOP YOU.

WE DIDN'T EVEN REALIZE OUR BEHAVIOR WAS FORCING YOU INTO A FANTASY WORLD.

I MEAN, HOW DID WE MISS THAT? YOU'RE MUCH TOO OLD TO PLAY WITH PUPPETS.

DON'T WORRY. WE AREN'T GOING TO TAKE YOUR PUPPETS AWAY.

BUT WE DON'T WANT YOU TO LOSE SIGHT OF WHAT IS REAL.

AND WE JUST WANT YOU TO KNOW THAT WE AREN'T GOING TO MAKE YOU TAKE ALL THOSE LESSONS ANYMORE.

REALLY?

AND WE WANT YOU TO BRING *ALL* YOUR PUPPETS TO THE PARTY TONIGHT... WHEN JONATHAN AND I...

...REVEAL OUR TRUE SELVES TO OUR SO-CALLED FRIENDS.

WE'RE GOING TO NEED YOU THERE AS BACK-UP.

ABSOLUTELY!

LATER THAT NIGHT. MISTY'S PARTY.

OH MY GOODNESS...

HERE, LET ME PASS AROUND SOME CAKE.

ASA, LET'S HELP THEM.

AYE, LASS. GET ELDURA.

YOUNGLING, I DO NOT KNOW YOU, YET YOU HAVE AWAKENED ME INTO A WORLD OF CRUELTY.

WHY?!

ASA?

ELDURA, THERE IS LITTLE TIME TO EXPLAIN EXCEPT TO SAY THAT EVEN THOUGH YOUR POWERS ARE DIMINISHED, YOU CAN STILL USE THEM.

WE NEED THEM NOW.

COUGH COUGH COUGH

COUGH

FUOMMM

SSSKiRT

MISTY?

WE'VE NEVER SEEN YOU LOOK LOVELIER.

R-REALLY?

Chapter Eight

The Truth Teller

THE HINKLE HOUSE.

AUDREY.

AUDREY!

HUH!

CRASH!

WHAT JUST HAP—

HOW ARE YOU ABLE TO TALK WITHOUT MY HANDS?

OH MY GOSH!

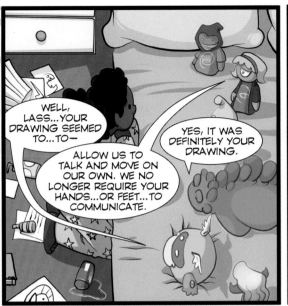

WELL, LASS...YOUR DRAWING SEEMED TO...TO—

YES, IT WAS DEFINITELY YOUR DRAWING.

ALLOW US TO TALK AND MOVE ON OUR OWN. WE NO LONGER REQUIRE YOUR HANDS...OR FEET...TO COMMUNICATE.

IT TOOK OVER THE ENTIRE ROOM, YEAH.

IT WAS QUITE LOVELY.

WELL, I FOR ONE THINK IT'S LOVELY WE CAN ALL TALK TO EACH OTHER NOW FREELY.

I'M NOT SAYING THAT RESTING ON YOUR FOOT WAS A BAD THING, *BUT* IT WAS STILL *YOUR FOOT*.

WHAT WERE YOU DRAWING, LASS?

WELL...I HAD THIS DREAM...AND THEN I STARTED DRAWING THIS... I DON'T KNOW WHAT ELSE TO CALL IT BUT... MAGIC CURRENTS...

...AND THEN I WAS BEING CHASED.

HERE.

IT STARTED HERE.

AND I REMEMBER...

...*YOU*, ASA!

I REMEMBER SEEING YOU WHEN I WAS VERY, VERY LITTLE. DO YOU REMEMBER ME FROM A VERY LONG TIME AGO?

NO, LASS. WHEN I FIRST CAME THROUGH THE PORTAL, AS I WAS CHANGING I REMEMBER A LARGE RED OBJECT. THEN...NOTHING.

I KNOW WHERE WE HAVE TO GO.

IS THIS WHAT YOU SAW?

BY FERGUS!

IT IS!

THIS IS VERY STRANGE—

CAN I HELP YOU, MISS?

OH... HEH... HELLO.

I WAS JUST LOOKING FOR SOMETHING.

I KNOW YOU...

...AND YOUR FRIEND.

96

SPOT! NO!

I GOT YOU, LASS.

THANKS, ASA!

WHEW!

GASP!

WHOOOMP!

98

CRACK!

ASA!

DON'T WORRY!

NIGHT

I DON'T KNOW HOW I CONVINCED TABITHA AND JONATHAN TO LET ME KEEP SPOT.

I ALSO DON'T KNOW HOW I DID IT, HOW I TRANSFORMED YOU, BUT I WISH I HAD DONE IT SOONER. AND I WISH I COULD GET YOU OUT OF YOUR PUPPET BODIES.

THAT'S OVER NOW, LASS, THANKS TO YOU. JUST KEEP TRYING.

IT WAS SOMETHING LIKE THIS.

I GUESS I'LL DO THIS THE OLD FASHIONED WAY.

HELLO, YOUR HIGHNESS.

WELL, TECHNICALLY YOUR MOTHER APPOINTED HERSELF QUEEN AND THEN TURNED EVIL, SO CALLING YOU A PRINCESS DOES SEEM KINDA QUESTIONABLE...

...BUT CONSIDERING HOW YOU'VE TURNED OUT, I SAY YOUR ROYAL TITLE IS ABSOLUTELY EARNED.

CERTAINLY, YOU ALL KNEW SHE WAS HEKLA'S DAUGHTER.

HOW ELSE WOULD A CHILD ANIMATE MERE TOYS?

DELFI, YOU ARE THE TRUTH TELLER, BUT I AM AFRAID YOUR SPEECH CONFUSES.

YEAH. I'M NOT SURE WHAT YOU ARE SAYING.

MY DEAR YOUNGLING...

...YOU ARE THE SECRET QUEEN HEKLA KEPT FROM THE NINE.

SHE KNEW THAT ONCE YOU CAME OF AGE, YOU WOULD BE VERY POWERFUL, AND THAT THE TWO OF YOU TOGETHER WOULD BE MORE POWERFUL THAN ANY OTHER BEINGS ON VORGON.

BUT AS YOU GREW MORE AWARE OF YOUR SURROUNDINGS, YOU GREW CURIOUS ABOUT US.

HEKLA DIDN'T WANT US TO KNOW ABOUT YOU. SHE DIDN'T WANT ANYONE TO.

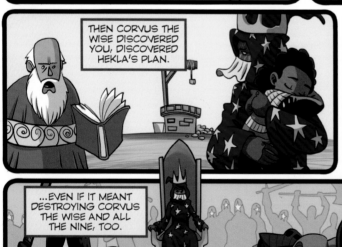

THEN CORVUS THE WISE DISCOVERED YOU, DISCOVERED HEKLA'S PLAN.

SHE VOWED TO PROTECT YOU AT ALL COSTS.

...EVEN IF IT MEANT DESTROYING CORVUS THE WISE AND ALL THE NINE, TOO.

YOUR MOTHER CHERISHED YOU.

BUT CORVUS THE WISE KNEW WHERE THE CHINKS WERE IN YOUR MOTHER'S MAGIC, AND SO HE PURSUED HER ACROSS VORGON AND WAITED UNTIL HEKLA'S POWERS WERE EXHAUSTED BEFORE HE MADE HIS MOVE.

IT WAS CORVUS THE WISE WHO TOOK YOU AWAY FROM YOUR MOTHER...

...FOUND A SAFE PLACE IN THIS WORLD TO SEND YOU SO THAT YOUR MOTHER COULD NOT TWIST YOU INTO A CREATURE MORE EVIL THAN SHE WAS.

BUT CORVUS DIDN'T REALIZE JUST HOW POWERFUL YOU ALREADY WERE.

IT WAS YOU WHO BROUGHT US TO THIS WORLD BECAUSE OF YOUR GREAT CURIOSITY ABOUT US.

NOT HEKLA.

NOT CORVUS THE WISE.

NOT ANY OTHER MAGICIAN ON VORGON.

IT WAS YOU...

...THE PRINCESS AUDRINA.

CAN YOU SPEAK TO US, LOVE?

LASS?

AUDREY?

AUDREY?

PRINCESS AUDRINA?

PRINCESS?

To be continued...

Seven down, two to go!

Fret not, Dear Reader, Audrey's adventures conclude in Book 3 as she unlocks the mysteries surrounding the rest of the Magic Nine AND the mysterious land of Vorgon!

BONUS STORY ONE
Ferocious Memory

Story by
Michelle Wright

Art by
Tracy Bailey

SO, IT WAS JUST ME AND THE TROLLUCK.

TROLLUCKS ARE GREEDY CREATURES THAT LIKE TO EAT THE YOUNGLINGS IN MY LAND—THE VOLCANIC REGION OF VORGON.

CLEARLY I *HAD* TO TEACH ONE A LESSON AND PUT AN END TO ITS TERRIBLE APPETITE.

SO, I LURED ONE AWAY FROM MY VILLAGE.

...AND THROUGH THE VALLEY...

...BUT THEN WE RAN INTO SOME TROUBLE.

BAP!

THE TROLLUCK WASN'T MUCH OF A TRACKER AND NEEDED SOME ENCOURAGEMENT.

BUT THE PROPER INCENTIVE HELPED ME SPRING MY PLAN.

I FLAMED HIM.

YOWL!

AND DID I EVER.

I HAD NEVER BEFORE FLAMED AN OPPONENT SO BRILLIANTLY OR COMPLETELY BEFORE.

I SORT OF FELT SORRY FOR HIM.

BUT THEN I REMEMBERED HOW MANY YOUNGLINGS HE HAD EATEN, AND THEN I DIDN'T FEEL SO BAD...

...EVEN THOUGH HE DID SEEM NAKED WITHOUT HIS BEARD AND EYEBROWS.

I THOUGHT THAT MY WORK WAS DONE...

...THAT I HAD TAUGHT THE TROLLUCK A LESSON HE WOULDN'T SOON FORGET.

BUT I WAS WRONG.

THE TROLLUCK WAS UNDETERRED.

GASP!

AND HE RENEWED HIS PLANS WITH FRIGHTENING FEROCITY.

I ONLY HAD TIME TO FIREBALL HIM SO I COULD ESCAPE.

AND I THOUGHT...

..."SURELY, THIS'LL DO THE TRICK."

THEN I NOTICED THAT SOMETHING WAS DIFFERENT ABOUT THIS TROLLUCK.

HE SEEMED TO FORGET THE EVENT THAT HAD JUST TRANSPIRED.

AND HE EVEN SEEMED TO HAVE FORGOTTEN ME ENTIRELY JUST AFTER A FEW SECONDS...

...SO HE ATTACKED ME AGAIN...

...AND AGAIN...

...AND AGAIN...

...UNTIL I FELT MY TREATMENT OF THE POOR CREATURE WAS CRUEL.

PANT PANT PANT

114

I DECIDED TO HELP THE TROLLUCK BY LURING HIM BACK HOME.

BUT THAT WAS EASIER SAID THAN DONE...

...ESPECIALLY SINCE THE BEING I WAS TRYING TO HELP HAD SERIOUS MEMORY PROBLEMS.

La-Dee Dee-Dee -Dee-Dee

HEY YOU! TROLLUCK!

BUT WE MADE HEADWAY...

...UNTIL WE FINALLY FOUND THE TROLLUCK'S PEOPLE.

OH, EARLING, WE WERE SO WORRIED.

DON'T EVER WANDER OFF AGAIN!

THEY WERE VERY THANKFUL, BUT I DIDN'T EXPECT MUCH FROM THEM IN THE WAY OF GRATITUDE.

THANK YOU TO SUCH A KIND AND CONSIDERATE—

AND TASTY!

WELL, YES, SHE DOES LOOK RATHER TASTY.

TROLLUCKS WILL BE TROLLUCKS AFTER ALL.

BUT THAT'S A STORY FOR ANOTHER DAY.

End.

BONUS STORY TWO

Naja's Quest

Story by
Michelle Wright

Art by
Tracy Bailey

FRIEND...

...WHAT IS YOUR JOURNEY?

DO YOU QUEST FOR MAGIC BEINGS?

DO YOU SEARCH FOR THE PERFECT LINE? THE PERFECT WORD?

FOR WHATEVER YOU SEARCH, START NOW BECAUSE YOU MAY MISS WHAT IT IS YOU WANT TO FIND OR WHAT IS MEANT TO FIND YOU.

OR YOU MAY TURN AWAY FROM IT BECAUSE YOU ARE TOO SCARED...

...OR YOU THINK THE JOURNEY TOO HARD.

BUT NO MATTER HOW DIFFICULT THE GOAL...

...IT IS WORTH EVERY BIT OF YOUR STRENGTH AND COURAGE TO CONTINUE...

...SINCE YOU MAY DISCOVER MUCH MORE THAN YOU INTENDED, AS I DID.

YOU SEE, I WAS TASKED BY MY ELDERS—AS ARE ALL YOUNGLINGS OF MY PEOPLE, THE NYXIUM—TO FIND AND COLLECT THE RARE BETONICA FLOWER ON THE SINGLE NIGHT OF THE YEAR THAT IT BLOOMS FOR ONLY A MINUTE...

...ON A NIGHT IN THAT LAND OF PERPETUAL DARK WHEN THE MOONS HAVE WANED AND CLOUDS COVER THE STARS, AND THERE IS NO LIGHT TO KEEP THE BETONICA'S PETALS SEALED.

YOU SEE, WHAT MADE THE BETONICA SO RARE A DELIGHT WAS THAT IT WAS THE EXACT COLOR OF THE DARKEST NIGHT, SO IT ONLY OPENED WHEN THE SKY MATCHED ITS HUE.

MANY YOUNG NYXIUM MISSED IT.

BUT THE ONES WHO WERE STEADFAST AND LUCKY ENOUGH TO FIND IT...

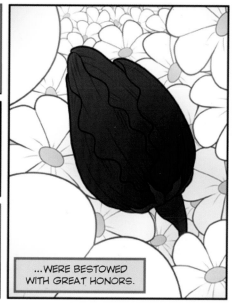

...WERE BESTOWED WITH GREAT HONORS.

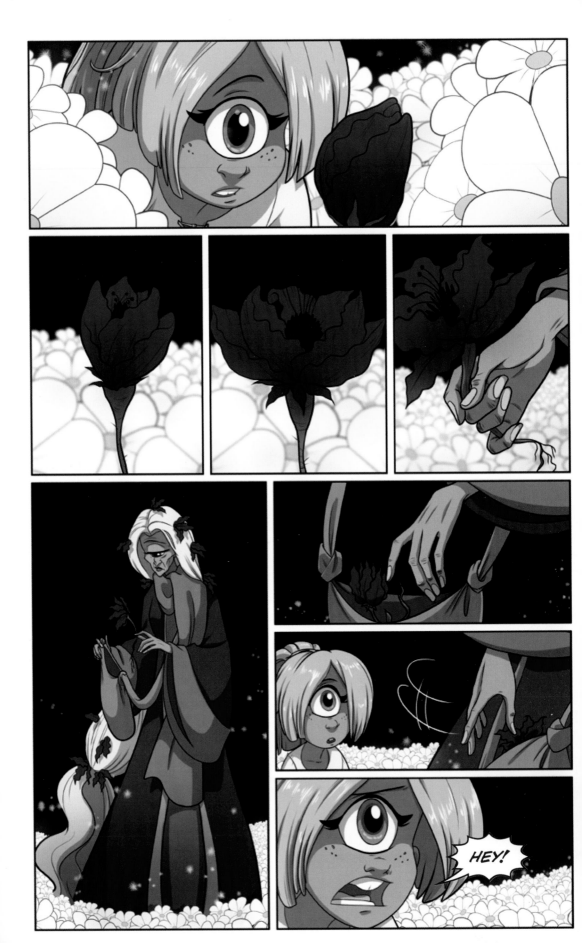

WHY DID YOU DO THAT?

THERE'S ANOTHER ONE?

AND ANOTHER?

YOU THOUGHT THERE WAS ONLY ONE?

YES.

WELL, YOU WERE WRONG.

THAT WAS A STORY I SPREAD TO—

DON'T!

YOU SEE, THE BETONICA KEEP ME ALIVE.

EVERY TIME ONE OF YOU YOUNGLINGS TAKE ONE FOR INITIATION, I LOSE LIFE.

I'M SORRY. I DIDN'T KNOW.

NO ONE KNOWS. NO ONE REMEMBERS WHAT SACRIFICES OUR PEOPLE FIRST MADE TO SURVIVE IN THIS DARK COUNTRY.

YOU SEE, THE BETONICA WERE ONCE SO PLENTIFUL AND POISONOUS THAT THEY THREATENED THE FIRST SETTLERS' WELL-BEING.

I CHOSE TO PROTECT MY PEOPLE FROM THE DANGER BY HARVESTING THE BETONICA, SPREADING STORIES ABOUT ITS POWERS TO KEEP MY KIN AWAY.

I THOUGHT I WOULD DIE IN THE PROCESS, BUT INSTEAD, I GREW IMMUNE AND THEN MY LIFE BECAME ENTWINED WITH THIS LITTLE FLOWER. WE CANNOT BE SEPARATED NOW.

AS I LOOKED AT THE OLD WOMAN, I REALIZED I HAD FOUND SOMETHING FAR MORE SPECIAL THAN A MERE MAGICAL FLOWER. I HAD FOUND LEGEND.

YOU ARE ONE OF *THE FIRST*.

HERE, TAKE THIS FOR YOUR INITIATION. IT WON'T DO MUCH DAMAGE.

WHAT I THOUGHT HAD BEEN THE PURPOSE OF MY JOURNEY WAS REPLACED WITH A FAR MORE IMPORTANT ONE.

NO.

I HAD THE RESPONSIBILITY OF REMINDING MY PEOPLE ABOUT THEIR PAST...

...A RESPONSIBILITY SO IMPORTANT THAT I NEVER WOULD HAVE DISCOVERED IT HAD I NOT BEGUN MY QUEST.

SO BELIEVE ME, FRIEND.

THE TIME TO START YOUR OWN QUEST IS NOW.

End.

BONUS STORY THREE
Love

**Story by
Michelle Wright**

**Art by
Tracy Bailey**

GOOD MORNING! HOW IS EVERYONE?

I LOVE HAVING A NEW FRIEND.

AND I LOVE FINDING OLD ONES.

I LOVE—

ARAAAAHH!

OPON, WHAT'S THE MATTER?

THERE.

A DUST BUNNY?

IT CAN'T HURT YOU.

IT CAN DO FAR WORSE.

WHAT DO YOU MEAN?

I'D RATHER NOT TALK ABOUT IT.

TAP TAP

IT'S JUST TOO DIFFICULT.

AW, C'MON, OPON. IT'S ALL RIGHT.

TAP TAP

WELL, FOR ONE THING, THEY'RE NOT CALLED "DUST BUNNIES" ON VORGON.

THEY'RE CALLED "LOVELIES."

LOVELIES? THAT DOESN'T SOUND SO BAD.

IT IS BAD.

IN FACT, IT'S TERRIBLE BECAUSE THEY DON'T HURT YOU.

LOVE!

THEY LOVE YOU.

GASP!

LOVE!

THEY LOVE YOU SO MUCH, THEY MULTIPLY OVER...

...AND OVER AS MANY TIMES AS IT TAKES TO SHOW YOU HOW MUCH THEY LOVE YOU.

LOVE!

AND IF YOU SHAKE THEM OFF...

...THE JUST LOVE YOU MORE.

LOVE! LOVE! LOVE!

I NEVER KNEW LOVE COULD BE SO FRIGHTENING.

126

OPON? SON...ARE YOU...

UNFORTUNATELY, ONCE THE LOVELIES GOT YOU...

...OK?

...THERE'S NO WAY TO RID YOURSELF OF THEM...

...EXCEPT ONE:

TO HELP THEM FIND A NEW LOVE INTEREST.

LOVE?

YOU SEE THE DIFFICULT PART OF THE WHOLE EXPERIENCE WASN'T BEING LOVED BY ALL THOSE LOVELIES...

IT WAS KNOWING THAT I WILLINGLY SENT THEM TO MY FATHER...

...WHO SENT THEM TO MY MOM...WHO SENT THEM TO THE NEIGHBORS...AND ON AND ON UNTIL THE LOVELIES HAD MOVED AWAY.

AUDREY, WHAT ARE YOU DOING?

YOU'LL SEE.

THERE YOU GO. ALL GONE!

End.

BONUS STORY FOUR

A Note On Cowardice

Story by
Michelle Wright

Art by
Tracy Bailey

THE TRUTH I HAVE TOLD THIS YOUNGLING TROUBLES HER.

I WISH IT WEREN'T SO, BUT TRUTH IS LIKE THAT.

WHEN IT APPEARS, WE OFTEN HAVE TO WRESTLE WITH IT, ACCEPT IT NO MATTER HOW PAINFUL IT MIGHT BE.

I, FOR ONE, FOUND MY *TRUTH* VERY DIFFICULT TO ACCEPT.

YOU SEE, I AM A COWARD.

ON VORGON, I WAS AFRAID OF WEATHER.

I WAS AFRAID OF SEBITS.

HEY! I LOVE YOU.

I WAS AFRAID OF LOVE.

I WAS EVEN AFRAID OF MY GRANDMOTHER WHO LIKED TO PINCH MY CHEEKS VERY HARD AND TELL ME CREEPY STORIES ABOUT WHEN SHE WAS A YOUNGLING.

YOU GET BACK HERE, MISSY.

I WAS SO AFRAID OF EVERYTHING THAT I RAN AWAY FROM MY VILLAGE...

...AND INTO A CAVE. I WAS EVEN AFRAID OF IT FOR A WHILE...

...BUT I FOUND THE DARK AND THE SILENCE PREFERABLE TO THE WIDER WORLD.

I MIGHT BE THERE STILL, HAD I NOT DISCOVERED THAT THE CAVE ALREADY HAD AN OCCUPANT, A MOST INTERESTING AND INSTRUCTIVE ONE.

EXCUSE ME. I REQUIRE SOME ASSISTANCE. WOULD YOU MIND?

NOW, DON'T BE ALARMED.

GASP!

I AM QUITE FRIGHTENING, BUT I DON'T MEAN YOU ANY HARM. ON ANOTHER DAY, YEAH SURE, I WOULD MEAN YOU A LOT OF HARM, BUT YOU CAUGHT ME ON A BAD DAY—

OH, GREAT. HERE IT COMES.

YEAH, YEAH.

AAAAAAAAAAAAAAHHH!!!

OK, GOT THAT OUT OF YOUR SYSTEM? GOOD.

YES, I AM THE CAVE DELLUS, WHO WOULD HAPPILY EAT YOU, BUT AS YOU CAN SEE...

...I FELL IN A STICKER PATCH, AND I AM IN QUITE A BIT OF PAIN AND A LITTLE FREAKED OUT AS WELL BECAUSE I HATE STICKERS, I MEAN, I HATE THEM. YOU'RE JUST WALKING ALONG, NOT EXPECTING ANYTHING, THEN—*BAM!*—STICKER PATCH.

YOU KNOW WHAT I MEAN?

Y-Y-YEAH...

PERFECT! WE'RE ON THE SAME PAGE.

PLEASE PROCEED.

AND SO, FOR ONCE, I DEALT WITH MY FEAR, AND CAREFULLY—VERY CAREFULLY—HELPED THE DELLUS.

...UNDERSTAND HOW I GOT A STICKER ON MY EYE, DO YOU?

NO.

WHEW!

THAT WAS SOMETHING ELSE.

YEAH.

YOU KNOW, IF YOU HAVE A FEW MINUTES, I'D LOVE FOR YOU TO STAY AND CHAT.

NOW, DON'T GET ME WRONG, I WAS TERRIFIED ALL THE SAME, BUT I LEARNED TO ACCEPT THE DELLUS FOR WHAT IT WAS.

WELL...I...*ER*...I NEED TO—

AW, *C'MON!*

O-O-KAY. SURE, WHY NOT?

OH, THANK YOU!

YOU DON'T KNOW HOW LONELY I'VE BEEN!

THERE, THERE.

IT'S OK.

MANY, *MANY* HOURS LATER.

AND THEN...I JUST THOUGHT, "WHAT AM I DOING? WHAT AM I DOING WITH *MY LIFE?* IS *THIS* WHO I AM MEANT TO BE?"

I KNOW. IT IS VERY HARD TO ACCEPT WHO WE REALLY ARE.

GOSH! THIS HAS *REALLY* HELPED.

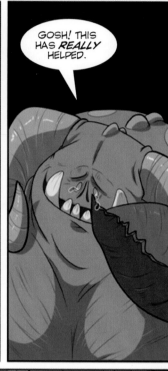

I'M GLAD.

BUT YOU KNOW...

...I THINK I *WILL* EAT YOU NOW.

HEY!

I ALSO LEARNED THAT MY TRUTH—WHO I REALLY WAS—WASN'T ALL THAT BAD.

ALL THAT RUNNING AWAY HAD SHARPENED MY INSTINCTS AND MADE ME A REALLY FAST RUNNER.

I HOPE MY DEAR PRINCESS AUDRINA WILL FIND THE SAME WAY WITH HER OWN TRUTH. IN FACT, I KNOW SHE WILL.

End.

Audrey's Magic Nine
Pin-Up Art

Huddleston • Moussa • Garcia

Huddleston • Moussa • Garcia

Huddleston • Moussa • Garcia

Huddleston • Moussa • Garcia

Huddleston • Gerbino • Garcia

Bonus Art

By Courtney Huddleston

MICHELLE WRIGHT

Michelle Wright's first love was the unicorn, and she has spent her life thus far trying to find her very own. Along the way, she has funded her exploration by working as an editor, a fiction writer, a comic book writer, an academic essayist, and a university lecturer after earning a Ph.D. from the University of Southern Mississippi's Center for Writers. She has been published in a wide variety of literary journals, including *Story South*, *Louisiana Literature*, **PANK**, and *Bitter Oleander*, and she has written a book chapter in the scholarly edition, *How Sefi Atta Illuminates African Culture and Tradition*. Her work in comic books includes *Li'l Red Stitch* and *Decoy: Origins*. Wright lives with her husband, the poet and essayist William Wright, and their fractious dog, Poppy, in Marietta, Georgia. Along with Poppy, she searches the North Georgia mountains for a unicorn, but Wright has the sneaking suspicion that their mythical pursuits have decidedly different purposes. Wright wants a unicorn as a second house pet, Poppy would like to eat one.

COURTNEY HUDDLESTON

Before he was the artist and creator of such fanciful comics as *A Bit Haywire*, *The Bully's Bully*, *Decoy*, and *Luci Phurr's Imps*, or the talented Project Coordinator at Penny-Farthing Productions, or even an adventurous world traveler with a penchant for wearing kilts and eating Swiss fondue, **Courtney Huddleston** was a precocious young storyteller who regaled his mother with imaginative tales while dangling upside down from a concrete stairwell in Tupelo, Mississippi. His love for creating and encouraging creativity in emerging talent, has never waned. Nor has his love for dangling from dangerous stairwells. He currently lives in Houston, Texas, with his wife Brandee, a first-grade teacher, and their two daughters, in a one-story house devoid of stairs of any kind.

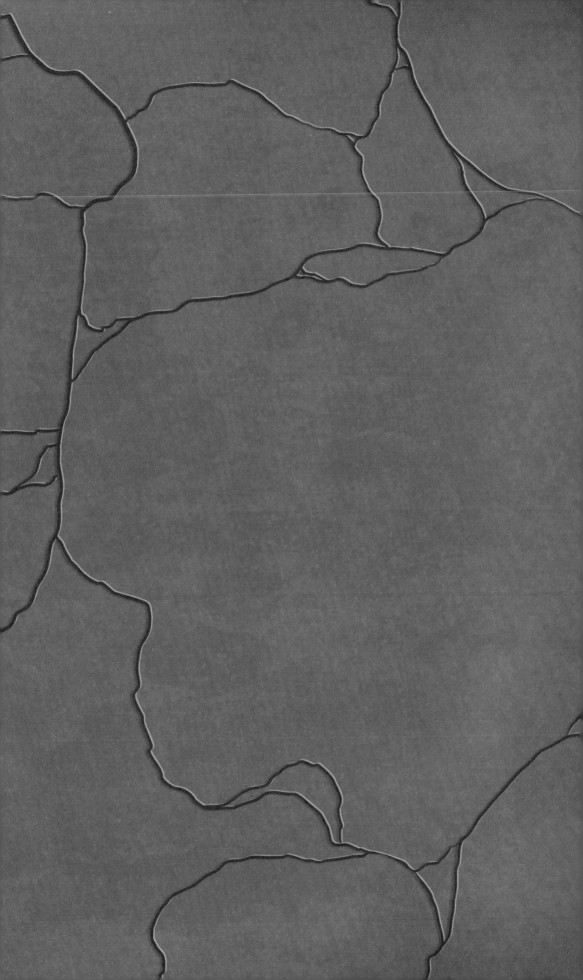

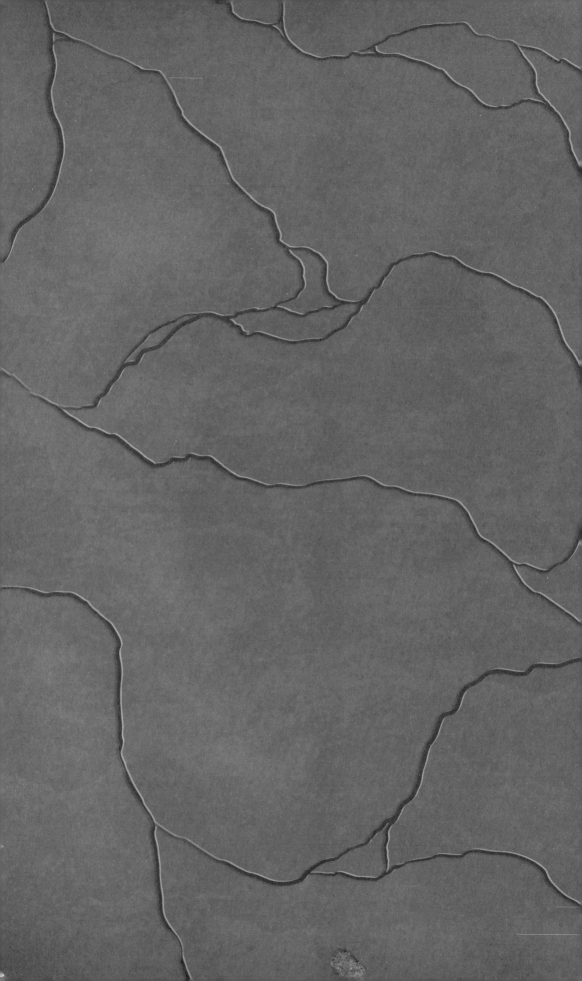

OCEANS ALIVE

Octopuses

by Ann Herriges

BELLWETHER MEDIA • MINNEAPOLIS, MN

Note to Librarians, Teachers, and Parents:

Blastoff! Readers are carefully developed by literacy experts and combine standards-based content with developmentally appropriate text.

Level 1 provides the most support through repetition of high-frequency words, light text, predictable sentence patterns, and strong visual support.

Level 2 offers early readers a bit more challenge through varied simple sentences, increased text load, and less repetition of high-frequency words.

Level 3 advances early-fluent readers toward fluency through increased text and concept load, less reliance on visuals, longer sentences, and more literary language.

Whichever book is right for your reader, Blastoff! Readers are the perfect books to build confidence and encourage a love of reading that will last a lifetime!

This edition first published in 2007 by Bellwether Media.

No part of this publication may be reproduced in whole or in part without written permission of the publisher. For information regarding permission, write to Bellwether Media Inc., Attention: Permissions Department, Post Office Box 1C, Minnetonka, MN 55345-9998.

Library of Congress Cataloging-in-Publication Data
Herriges, Ann.
  Octopuses / by Ann Herriges.
    p. cm. — (Blastoff! readers) (Oceans alive!)
Summary: "Simple text and supportive images introduce beginning readers to octopuses. Intended for students in kindergarten through third grade."
  Includes bibliographical references and index.
  ISBN-10: 1-60014-019-X (hardcover : alk. paper)
  ISBN-13: 978-1-60014-019-8 (hardcover : alk. paper)
  1. Octopuses—Juvenile literature. I. Title. II. Series. III. Series: Oceans alive!

  QL430.3.O2H47 2006
  594'.56—dc22   2006002771

Text copyright © 2007 by Bellwether Media.
Printed in the United States of America.

Table of Contents

Octopuses have soft bodies.

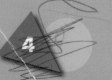
4

They can fit their bodies
through small spaces.

5

eyes

Octopuses have a head.

They have two large eyes.

Octopuses have eight arms.

There are **webs** of skin
between the arms.

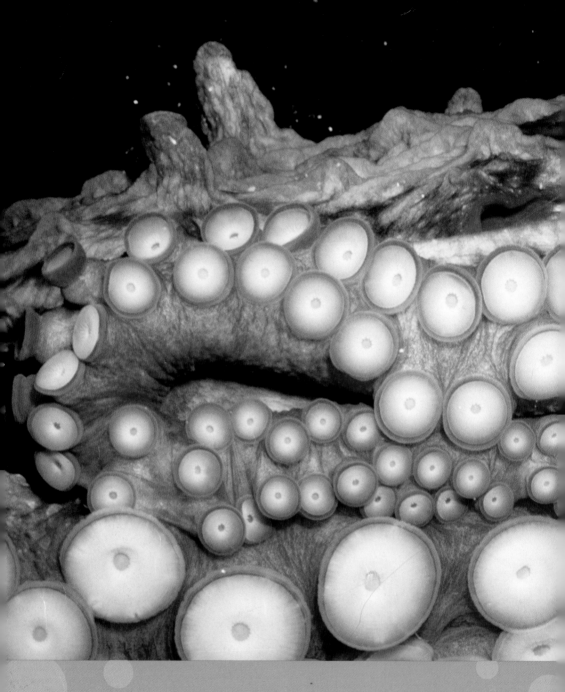

Octopus arms have **suckers**.

10

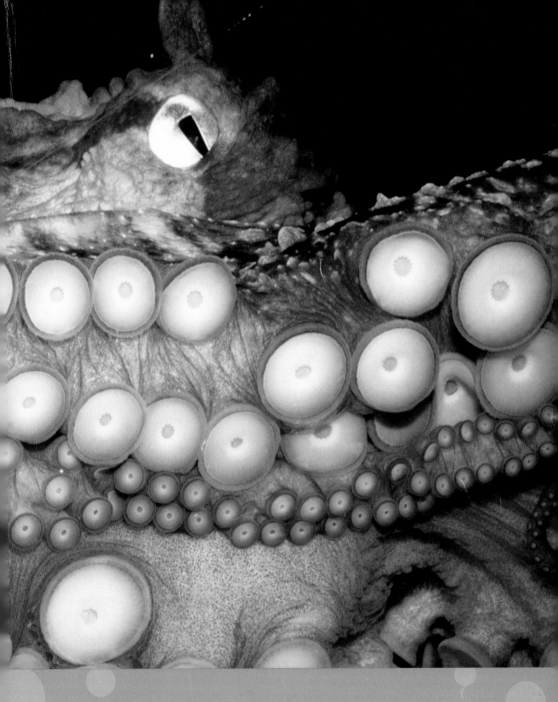

Octopuses use their suckers
to smell and to taste.

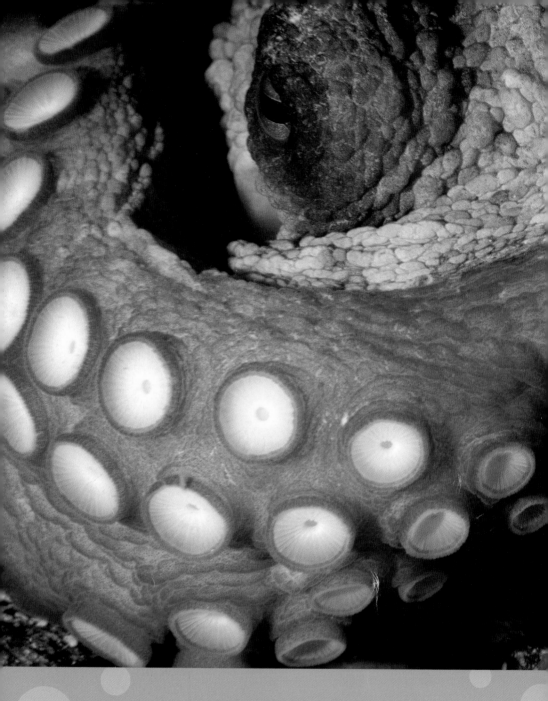

Octopuses also use the suckers to grab things and to hold onto rocks.

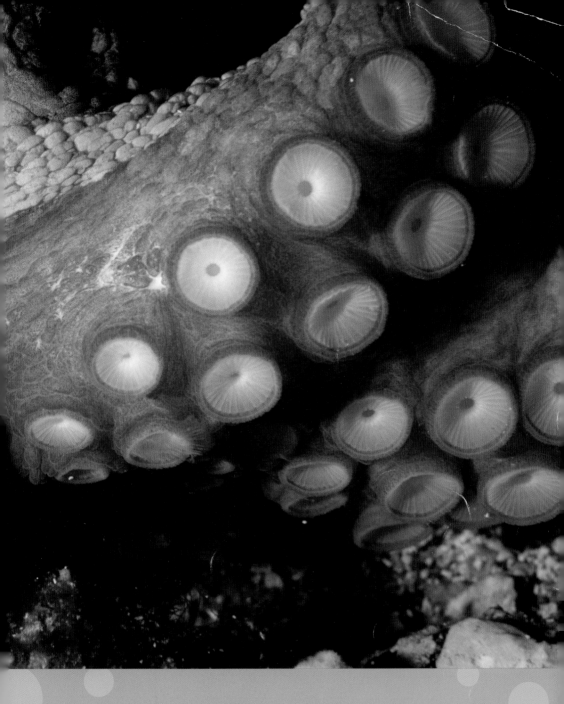

They use their suckers to crawl on the ocean floor.

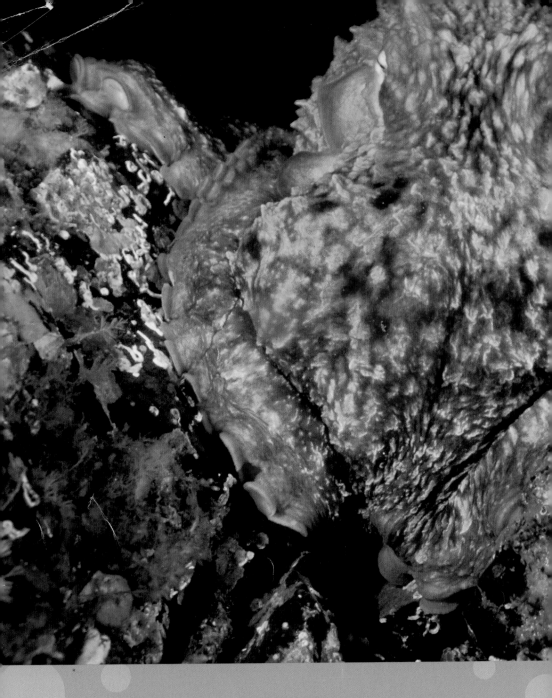

Octopuses live alone in rocky **dens**.

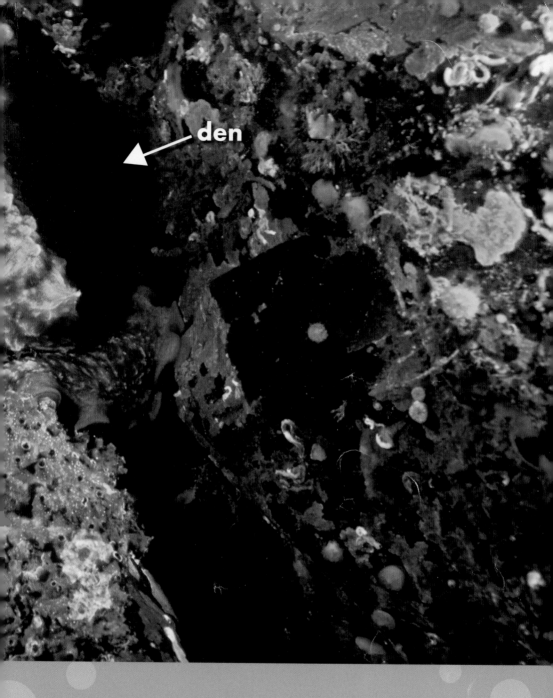

den

They leave their dens to
hunt for crabs, clams,
and lobsters.

15

Octopuses poke their arms between rocks to search for their **prey**.

16

They bring the prey back to
their dens to eat.

Octopuses hide
from **predators**.

They can change color to match their **surroundings**.

An octopus can squirt dark **ink** into the water. This surprises a predator.

Swoosh! The octopus
escapes. It changes color
and swims away.

Glossary

den—an animal's home; octopuses make their dens between rocks or inside coral caves; sometimes they build their own dens.

ink—a dark liquid that octopuses can squirt from their bodies

predator—an animal that hunts other animals for food; seals, whales, and eels are some of the predators that eat octopuses.

prey—an animal that is hunted by another animal for food; octopuses eat crabs, clams, snails, and lobsters; some octopuses eat other octopuses.

suckers—round cup-shaped parts on an octopus's arms; suckers can bend and stretch to hold onto things.

surroundings—the area around something; the octopus can change its color to match the plants, rocks, and coral around it.

web—the fold of skin between the arms of an octopus

To Learn More

AT THE LIBRARY

Andreae, Giles. *Commotion in the Ocean*. Wilton, Conn.: Tiger Tales, 2002.

Langeland, Deirdre. *Octopus' Den*. Norwalk, Conn.: Soundprints, 1997.

Most, Bernard. *My Very Own Octopus*. New York: Harcourt Brace Jovanovich, 1980.

Pitcher, Caroline. *Nico's Octopus*. New York: Crocodile Books, 2003.

Roop, Connie. *Octopus Under the Sea*. New York: Scholastic, 2001.

Tate, Suzanne. *Oozey Octopus: A Tale of a Clever Critter*. Nags Head, N.C.: Nags Head Art, 2000.

Wallace, Karen. *Gentle Giant Octopus*. Cambridge, Mass.: Candlewick Press, 1998.

ON THE WEB
Learning more about octopuses is as easy as 1, 2, 3.

1. Go to www.factsurfer.com

2. Enter "octopuses" into search box.

3. Click the "Surf" button and you will see a list of related web sites.

With factsurfer.com, finding more information is just a click away.

Index

The photographs in this book are reproduced through the courtesy of: Stuart Westmorland/Getty Images, front cover; Steven Hunt/Getty Images, pp. 4-5; Aqua Image/Alamy, pp. 6-7; David Fleetham/Getty Images, pp. 8-9, 14-15; Ken Lucas/Getty Images, pp. 10-11; Lionel Isy-Schwart/Getty Images, pp. 12-13; Brandon Cole Marine Photography/Alamy, pp. 16-17; Reinhard Dirscherl/Alamy, pp. 18-19; Jeff Rotman/Alamy, pp. 20-21.